This
PJ BOOK
belongs to

_____

_____

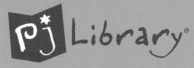

JEWISH BEDTIME STORIES and SONGS

Dedicated to
Alex Cohen

The artwork was done
using watercolor, Gouache,
pencil, ink and collage.

VIKING
Published by the Penguin Group
Penguin Putnam Books for Young Readers, 345 Hudson Street, New York, New York, 10014, U.S.A.
Penguin Books Ltd, 27 Wrights Lane, London, W8 5TZ, England
Penguin Books Australia Ltd, Ringwood, Victoria, Australia
Penguin Books Canada Ltd, 10 Alcorn Avenue, Toronto, Ontario, Canada M4V 3B2
Penguin Books (N.Z.) Ltd, 182-190 Wairau Road, Auckland 10, New Zealand
Penguin Books Ltd, Registered Offices: Harmondsworth, Middlesex, England
First published in 1977 by Random House, Inc.

This edition with new illustrations published in 1999 by Viking, a member of
Penguin Putnam Books for Young Readers

7 9 10 8

Copyright © Simms Taback, 1999
All rights reserved

LIBRARY OF CONGRESS CATALOGING-IN-PUBLICATION DATA
Taback, Simms. Joseph had a little overcoat / by Simms Taback. p. cm.
Summary: A very old overcoat is recycled numerous times into a variety of garments.
ISBN 978-0-670-87855-0 (hardcover)
Special Markets ISBN 978-0-670-01186-5
[1. Coats-Fiction. 2. Clothing and dress-Fiction.] I. Title.
PZ7.T1115Jo 1999 [E]-dc21 98-47721 CIP AC

Welcome40K2/B0942/All ages
Printed in China
All lettering designed by Simms Taback

Joseph Had a Little Overcoat

He wore the coat for a long time and then something happened to it.

(and there's a moral, too!)

Simms Taback

Viking

ttle overcoat. It was old and worn.

So he made a jacket out of it

and went to the fair.

Joseph had a little jacket. It got old and worn.

and danced at his nephew's wedding.

Joseph had a little vest. It got old and worn.

So he made a scarf out of it

and sang in the men's chorus.

Joseph had a little scarf. It got old and worn.

and went to visit his married sister in the city.

Joseph had a little necktie. It got old and worn.

and drank a glass of hot tea with lemon.

and used it to fasten his suspenders.

Joseph had a little button. One day he lost it.

Now he had nothing.

What one has,
one doesn't want,
and what one wants,
one doesn't have.

you can always make something out of nothing.

Dear Readers,

    As a child I had a favorite song - a yiddish folk song called "I Had a Little Overcoat." Many years ago, I adapted the song to make a book and I called it <u>Joseph Had a Little Overcoat</u>. Some people noticed that Joseph looked a lot like me.

    Now you know that no artist is ever satisfied with his work, but usually we don't get to do it over. So I am particularly happy to be publishing this newly illustrated version of Joseph. I hope that all of you who wrote to me about the early version will take this one to your hearts. That would prove that "you can always make something out of nothing"... over and over again!

Simms Taback

I Had a Little Overcoat (Hob Ich Mir a Mantl)

With some help from Evy Silverman, Lisa Deane, Bert Silverman, Janet Pascal and Sidor Belarsky

(1) I had a lit-tle o-ver-coat, much too old to sew, La la la la la la la la la la la.(1)What-
(2) had a lit-tle jack-et, much too old to sew, (2)What-
(3) had a lit-tle vest, — much too old to sew, (3)What-
(4) had a lit-tle tie, — much too old to sew, (4)What-
(5) had a lit-tle but-ton, where ev-er did it go, (5)What-
(6) All I had was no-thing, and no-thing much to sew, (6)What

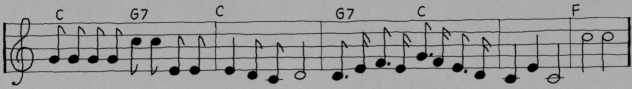

(1) ev-er could I do with it, I just did-n't know. La la la la la la la la la la la, So I
(2) ev-er could I do with it,
(3) ev-er could I do with it,
(4) ev-er could I do with it,
(5) ev-er did I do with it,
(6) could I do with no-thing,

thought what could I do(1)and made my-self a jack-et that was al-most new, La la la la la la la
(2)and made my-self a vest — that was al-most new.
(3)and made my-self a tie — that was al-most new.
(4)and made my-self a but-ton that was al-most new.
(5)but all I had was noth-ing nei-ther old or new.
(6)and sang my-self a song and I sing this song to you.

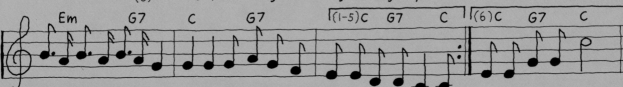

la la la la la la la la(1)made my-self a jack-et that was al-most new. I sing this song to you.
(2)made my-self a vest — that was al-most new. I
(3)made my-self a tie — that was al-most new. I
(4)made my-self a but-ton that was al-most new. I
(5)all I had was noth-ing nei-ther old or new. —
(6)sang my-self a song and I